Silvia Hilli Weber

Little Lu

 ZONDERkidz

ZONDERVAN.com/
AUTHORTRACKER
follow your favorite authors

There once was a young
giraffe named Lulatch.

But because she was still so
small, everyone called her
Little Lu.

One morning, Little Lu woke up and noticed that something was not right. She had a knot in her neck!

"How did this happen? And how do I fix it?" Little Lu was frightened. She looked around for someone to help her. Where was her mother?

A small sparrow saw Lu and fluttered around her neck. "What do you have there?" asked the bird.

"My neck's in a knot, and I don't know how to get it out," the small giraffe grumbled.

"Maybe you should wrap a scarf around your neck," suggested the sparrow, "and keep the knot warm."

"But I'm not cold!" Lu said to herself.

Nevertheless, she wound a long scarf around her neck. She waited a while and checked to see if she was better, but the knot was still there.

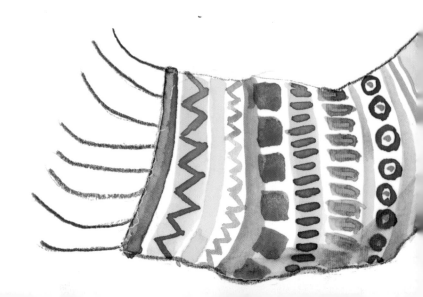

Sometime later, a rabbit hopped past. He took one look at the little giraffe's neck and stammered, "You have s-s-something s-s-stuck in your th-th-throat!"

"Oh brother," murmured Lu. "Can't you see my neck is in a knot?"

The rabbit suggested timidly, "M-m-maybe if you hop on two legs and sh-sh-shake your head, it will come out."

"But I don't have water in my ear!" Lu said to herself. But she began to hop anyway. And still the knot remained.

Soon a little badger came by. He said, giggling, "Hey Little Lu, lookin' good today. Is that the newest giraffe style?"

"Very funny," said Lu. "How about you stop joking and help me get this knot out of my throat?"

The badger thought for a moment and said, "Take three big gulps of air and hold your breath."

But gulping air was not an easy task with a knot in her neck, so Little Lu just stood there. She didn't know what to do.

Finally, Little Lu's mama came by with breakfast. When she saw Lu, she said tenderly, "Oh my, you don't look well today, my little one."

Tears began to roll down Little Lu's face as she told her mama everything that had happened. Lu's mama listened and then carefully studied the knot in Lu's throat.

Lu tried to hold still while her mama untwisted the knot. And suddenly the knot was gone!

Lu was very relieved. Now they could have breakfast.

"Mama, why do giraffes have such long necks?" asked Little Lu.

Mama stroked Lu's neck and said kindly, "Because God made us this way."

"But the birds, the rabbits, and the badgers do just fine without long necks," said Little Lu.

"God has made each of us special. Badgers have strong claws to dig in the dirt. Rabbits have long ears so they can hear better. Sparrows have wings to fly. And giraffes have long necks so we can reach the highest leaves in the trees."

This made Lu happy, and she thanked God for giving giraffes the sweetest leaves in the trees.

God made the wild animals
according to their kinds, the
livestock according to their kinds,
and all the creatures that move
along the ground according to
their kinds. And God saw that it
was good.

—Genesis 1:25